AMNESIA

Naydin Rowland

A PSYCHOLOGICAL THRILLER

Amnesia

NAYDIN ROWLAND

Prologue

The two girls struggled with each other. They were on the cliffs. It was the middle of the night, raining and thundering. Perfect weather for a murder. One was waving a knife in her hand, trying to frighten the other one away, but she wouldn't be able to scare *her* away. She was a murderer. Despite the pain in her chest and stomach, she plunged the knife at the second girl. The second girl gasped and choked as her opponent sobbed and backed off. The girl she had just stabbed looked at her and laughed.

"What am I waiting for?" she thought, laughing louder to herself, "There's a cliff behind her. One good push and she's gone! Gone forever!"

She laughed again and charged toward her. The girl screamed and pushed the knife deeper into her skin. The second girl screamed in agony while the other girl grabbed the knife to pull it out, but as she did so, her wounded opponent gave her an almighty push and she fell. She heard the first girl scream as she plunged to her death. Just before the second girl passed out, she heard someone call her name. There was another girl standing at the entrance to the graveyard; she was looking at her accusingly. There was a crash not so far away; she could see the flames. A boy started to call her name, then he cried out different names. Names that the girl could not pay attention to. She fell, but unfortunately, the wrong way. She plummeted down to join her opponent on the rocks below. But there was a smile on her face as she remembered the people she had killed that night. Her mother, her father, her brother and her... She hit the ground.

Chapter 1

One year later

Lucinda Jordan woke up and looked around her bedroom. Everything was a pastel colour: lemon yellow, dusty rose, and baby blue. Lucinda screamed. She kept on screaming until a boy entered her room. A crutch in his hand, he limped towards her. He had the exact same hair as Justin Bieber, crystal blue eyes, and he was very tall and skinny, like a runner. Lucinda screamed louder. He really looked like a mix between Justin Bieber and Zac Efron. Not scary at all, cute in fact, but she had no idea who he was.

"Quiet!" he demanded, though he said it lovingly. "Lucinda, quiet. You're okay."

"Where am I?" she choked out.

"You're home, Luce, you're home. You're in your bedroom. You live here. Number eighteen, Honeysuckle Lane. Remember?" said Trey, wrapping his arms around her and kissing her forehead.

Lucinda shook her head, trying to shrug this strange boy off. "I don't remember anything! Who are you?"

"The doctor feared this," he murmured. "Lucinda, I am your older brother, Trey. Trey Jordan. I'm seventeen; I go to a college a few towns away from here. Do you remember?"

Lucinda shook her head. "Who am I?"

"You are Lucinda Jordan, my fifteen year old sister. Born the sixteenth of December 1995. You go to Burns High School here. Do you remember? We live in Canada. Does any of that ring a bell?"

"No," shivered Lucinda. Why couldn't she remember?

"Lucinda, you have amnesia. The doctor told me you might. I have no idea what happened that night we found you at the cliff. I thought you were dead for sure, but the doctor said you were alive. You've been in a coma for a year, but even though you were alive, I kept worrying that you would be in that coma forever. A year is a long time to wait for your sister to come back so you can see her happy, well, and alive again."

"The cliff?"

"The cliff near the graveyard. Like I said, I have no idea what happened to you there, but we found you at the bottom of the cliff. You'd die for sure if you fell, but miraculously, you survived, only to leave you battered, in a coma and to suffer with memory loss. Though it's tough for you and me to see yourself like this, I don't care, I'm just grateful that you are alive."

Lucinda shuddered. There were so many questions spinning around in her head. What had happened to her? How did she survive falling from a cliff? How had she fallen off? What was she doing on a cliff in the first place? Was she with Trey when she fell? Was she with *anyone*?

"Could you pass me a mirror, please?" she asked.

Trey passed her the mirror beside her, and Lucinda reached out for it with an aching arm. It was like she was making her first movements, like a baby the second it's born. Grabbing the mirror, she peered at her face. Her face was clear, but she screamed.

"What's wrong?" gasped Trey, worrying that she might be delusional.

"That's not me...is it?" she quivered.

"It is. It is you. You are Lucinda Jordan. Sparkling blue eyes with chocolate brown hair in a cute bob."

Lucinda stared into the mirror again, staring at her own face, her own face she didn't even recognise.

"Come on, get up and get ready, and I'll make you breakfast" said Trey, lovingly.

Lucinda nodded slowly and got up carefully. Her body felt weak and fragile, like a doll's. Like the many porcelain dolls in pretty little dresses that surrounded her room. Trey made sure she could stand properly and then limped to the kitchen to fix breakfast.

Lucinda peered inside her wardrobe. She frowned at the clothes. Is this what she wore before she got amnesia? Pretty little lacy things like the dolls? All boring colours like beige and grey or pastel colours like the ones painted on her bedroom walls? She instantly hated her clothing. But why? If this was what she wore before, why didn't she like it now? She slipped on some white trousers with a frilly beige top. She made her way slowly downstairs, looking around the house, trying to remember any of it. But of course, she couldn't.

Trey smiled as she entered the kitchen.

"I missed your fashion sense when you were in that coma. I always dreamed of you finally waking up when I least expected it, and I'd be sat in this kitchen and you'd give me the surprise of my life when you'd come sauntering in, wearing your soft, gentle clothes."

Lucinda smiled weakly and sat down the kitchen table. Trey placed a plate of pancakes in front of her, drowned in syrup. Lucinda stared at it.

"What's this?"

"This is your favourite thing to have at breakfast, Lucinda," stated Trey. "Don't you remember? I thought I'd make you your favourite for breakfast, you know, to celebrate."

Lucinda nodded and cut out a chunk of it and put it in her mouth. After she swallowed it, she smiled weakly and gratefully at Trey. Although Trey said it was her favourite food to have at breakfast, Lucinda could only take three bites before she gave up. It was too sickly sweet for her. It seemed like the Lucinda she had forgotten and left behind on the cliff was a little bit *too* sweet and sickly. Then she remembered something vital. If Trey was at college most of the time and Lucinda was fifteen...

"Where are our parents?" she asked

Trey stiffened at that question then bowed his head.

"They are dead. They died before you fell off the cliff. They died in a car crash. Hence my..."

He nodded to his leg.

"Was I in the car with you?"

"No. You were out watching a movie with your friends."

"What day is it today?" she asked, after she put down her knife and fork.

"Tuesday."

"That means I'll have to go to school."

"Of course it doesn't, Luce! You've just woken up from a coma! Nobody will expect you to go to school when you've just woken up from a coma!"

Lucinda nodded, wondering what her school was like. She tried to break a bit of the wall down that was keeping her memories captive, but she couldn't even leave a scratch on it. She couldn't remember a thing.

"Do I have any friends at school?"

"Of course. You have only a couple of best friends that you're always with, but you talk to *everyone* at school. You love them and they love you."

Lucinda nodded again and Trey looked down at her nearly full plate.

"Aren't you that hungry this morning? I thought you'd have shovelled that down. It's your favourite."

"So you said. But, no, I'm not really that hungry; I feel a little sick."

"Are you alright? Do you want to go back to bed?" asked Trey, all concern.

Lucinda shook her head. "No, I'm fine. I'll get over it. Tell me more about my friends."

Trey smiled, hoping that it might trigger her memory.

"You have four very close friends: Apple Ambrose, Helen Manson, India Peterson, and Callumn Hanks. They came to visit you when you were asleep. I'll have to phone them after school and tell them the good news!"

Lucinda nodded again. Trey nodded too. 'Funny,' Lucinda thought, 'how much a nod can say without opening your mouth to speak.'

"What are they like?" she asked.

Trey frowned. "Can't you remember your own friends?"

"Trey! I can't remember anything"

"Well...I don't know. I don't hang around with them or see them much because I'm not at high school anymore, but they seemed okay when they came round. Quiet, but then, they would be. They were really worried about you; they cried as soon as they saw you."

"That ugly am I?" laughed Lucinda. Trey smiled.

"I'm glad you've got your sense of humour back, Luce. It's so nice to hear your voice and your laugh again."

Lucinda nodded and retreated back to her pastel coloured room. Her sickly sweet, pastel coloured room.

Chapter 2

Lucinda's friends came to her house right after school. They were red in the face because they had rushed to get there; they couldn't wait to see their friend awake and well again.

India was the first to hug Lucinda.

"Oh Luce! I thought you would never wake up! The doctors said you would one day, but I never thought..." she gabbled.

"Well, I'm awake now," smiled Lucinda.

She studied India Peterson. She was dark-skinned and had very long, glossy black hair that she had in one long ponytail. Her eyes were huge and brown and even though she was still in her school clothes, Lucinda could tell she favoured dark colours. She had put an azure blue heavily on her eyes and her cheeks were almost crimson with all the blush she had put on.

Helen hugged her next and Lucinda could see she had tears in her hazel coloured eyes, but she

15

could also see her face and her caramel hair glow she was so happy.

Apple Ambrose was crying, but she was also laughing with relief. Lucinda smiled at her warmly and hugged her tightly.

"It's alright, Apple. Everything's alright. It doesn't matter that I've lost my memory; it's going to be fun remembering, right?"

Apple nodded, but didn't look so certain. Lucinda smiled at Apple again. Apple was very pretty. She had shoulder-length blonde hair, natural pink cheeks and turquoise coloured eyes, like the colour of the sea.

The last to hug Lucinda was Callumn Hanks. He was the shyest of the group and was quite short for a fifteen year old. He had spiky white hair and ice coloured eyes. His appearance seemed cold, like a snowman, but he was just very shy and restricted, not quite knowing where to put himself when it came to affection or conversations.

As Lucinda hugged each of her friends, she felt happy to meet more people, but she had no recollection of them. She would've had no idea who they were if she had gone to school and they had waved her over or said hello to her.

"Oh, are we *that* memorable and important to you?" laughed Helen.

Lucinda laughed. "I'm sorry."

"You...don't need to be s...sorry," stuttered Callumn. "It's not your...f...fault that you fell...off...off that cliff."

"Do you know what happened on the cliffs?" Lucinda asked.

The small group of friends looked at each other and then shook their heads.

"Alas, we don't," said Helen

"Was I up there with someone?" she asked, just to be curious.

Again the group of friends glanced at one another, only this time they shrugged their shoulders.

Lucinda sighed. How was she supposed to remember anything when no one knew what happened the night she had lost her memory?

"Anyway," started Helen, changing the subject and smiling bravely, "You've missed out on a lot of school work and..."

Trey groaned and rolled his eyes. "Honestly, Helen, she's just woke up from a *coma*! She doesn't want schoolwork to burden her, though I know she will have to go back to school sometime."

Lucinda smiled at Helen to show that she was grateful for the thought, but she really didn't feel like doing any work. Despite not remembering her own family, friends and past, she remembered her ABC and one, two, threes.

"But you should know better than anyone that Luce loves schoolwork," said Helen.

"Do I?" Lucinda asked, frowning thoughtfully.

Trey nodded but didn't suggest anything.

"Oh yes," agreed India. "You were always top in class. You helped me out with all that math homework one week."

Lucinda blinked. She couldn't remember that.

It was quiet for a moment and then Trey suggested that they should all go upstairs to get to know each other again.

The small group nodded and obediently went upstairs. As they made their way to Lucinda's bedroom, there was an awkward silence and Lucinda started to wonder how they had become friends and what they were like before she had had her accident, while the others glanced nervously around the house as if they were looking out for an evil spirit that lingered somewhere in the dark corners of the house.

Lucinda opened the door to her sickly sweet bedroom and led her small group of friends in. They seated themselves on her bed or on the stools scattered around the room like lemon and rose pink mushrooms. As soon as they all sat down, the tension seemed to cease and the atmosphere turned warm and happy.

"So...India... Is that your real name? India?"

India sighed. "Unfortunately, yes. I was born in India, so my parents called me that. They thought it would be nicer than calling me the capital of India. And so it is too! I guess I have to consider myself lucky. Just imagine how people would mock me if I had been born in England and I was called London, or born in America and I was called New York, or if I was born in Spain and called Madrid."

Lucinda giggled. "Actually, the capital of America is Washington D.C."

Everyone laughed at that.

"See, even though you've lost your memory...you haven't lost your intelligence or bbb...brightness," Callumn stated.

Lucinda smiled weakly at that.

"Actually, there are quite a lot of states in America that you can call children now," pointed out Apple. "Carolina, Louisiana, Virginia..."

"I don't think I'd like to be called Virginia," said India.

"Neither would I in truth," agreed Apple. "I think I'll just stick with Apple."

"Imagine if your parents called you peach or lemon or mango," giggled India.

Apple rolled her eyes. "This is what I get every time I mention my name," she whispered to Lucinda, but loud enough for all the others to hear. "I don't think Apple's such a silly name. I think it's quite sweet, but this lot tease me about it and I have to keep explaining that I was called it because mum got a craving on apples."

"Like I said, it's a good thing she didn't get a craving on mango or watermelon or some other fruit...or a veg!"

Apple laughed and then rolled her sea-green eyes again.

"How did we meet and make friends?" asked Lucinda, starting a new topic.

Helen jumped. "I know you have amnesia, Luce, but I expected you to at least remember how we all met!"

Lucinda shook her head sadly. "I can't remember anything, Helen. And I feel really sorry that I've forgotten all the good times we shared, all the jokes we cracked in the past and that we've laughed at, you know, those moments that we can't relive again."

Helen frowned sadly, but then turned her attention to the first day that they met at school.

"It was really funny. You were always intelligent and bright, but you were also very shy, being it the first day of high school. You asked me for directions and I said that I didn't know where to go either because I was new too! We were trailing around, trying to find our first class, then we bumped into Apple..."

Helen nodded at Apple, who smiled and blushed.

"...We found our way to our class, but all day we kept picking up people. Can you remember Steven? Steven Madge?"

Lucinda shook her head.

"We picked up Steven too, but...he died a while ago."

Helen looked down at the floor, and the others couldn't meet Lucinda's gaze either, as they shuffled their feet and sat in silence, remembering what had happened to him.

Lucinda raised her eyebrows in concern.

"Oh! Oh, I'm so sorry! What did he die of?"

Everyone gave each other uneasy glances and then India shook her head.

"No. It's too horrible to talk about, but don't beat yourself up over it. If you can't remember, then don't try. It's not important right now."

Lucinda nodded to show she understood, though she couldn't really.

"So we just stayed friends after that then?" asked Lucinda, after a short moment of silence.

Helen snapped out of her grief and smiled at her. "Yes. We did and have been going strong ever since."

Lucinda smiled. She was sure if she could remember, she would've been beaming at the memory, but in this situation, she'd beam at anything she remembered from the past.

Lucinda searched her brain for another question she could ask. Her brain was a bowl full of questions, so many questions, all she had to do was dip her hand into the bowl and pick one out.

"What about brothers and sisters? Do you have any brothers and sisters I'm close to?"

"I'm an only child," said Apple. "My mother died a few weeks after she gave birth to me, so I just live with my dad."

Apple sounded so mournful when she said that, Lucinda had to sympathize with her as if her mother had died yesterday.

"I know how you feel," comforted Lucinda. "My parents died in a car crash, which you all might know about anyway."

"Did Trey tell you that?" asked Apple

"Yes. Who else would? I've only seen him and all of you."

Apple nodded weakly.

"I have a brother that's the same age as Trey and two little sisters that have just started Primary School," said India. "You used to play with Paris quite a lot."

"Paris?" smiled Lucinda, raising a questioning brow.

India sighed. "Yes, like me, she is also an unfortunate that has been named after a place."

"What's your brother and your other sister called?"

"Rose and Buddy."

"Oh, well those aren't so bad," chuckled Lucinda.

"I, too, am a...am an only child," continued Callumn.

"Are you alright, Callumn?" asked Lucinda worriedly. She had noticed he pauses sometimes in his sentences, but she just thought that was because he was shy, but then she noticed that when he spoke it looked as though he was struggling to talk and it hurt to do so.

"Yes," jumped Callumn. "I'm...I'm fine. Why shouldn't I be?"

"You..."

Lucinda was about to mention the strain in his voice, but didn't have the heart to question him about it; he may have a breathing problem, asthma maybe. Lucinda waved her hand to show that she wanted to leave the matter.

They talked for a while more. Talking about old times, talking about the school and the work they were doing.

When it was time for them to leave, India begged to stay overnight, but Trey shook his head.

"Not tonight, India, sorry. It was only today that Lucinda woke up from a coma, you know. She needs her rest, she doesn't need all of you keeping her awake with your giggles in the middle of the night."

India scoffed and rolled her eyes.

"Please, Trey."

Trey raised his eyebrows and folded his arms. "Not tonight."

"It's not up to you, it's up to Lucinda. Lucinda should decide whether she's up for it or not."

They all looked at Lucinda to give them an answer and Lucinda stared back at them. Despite not wanting to disappoint her friends, she didn't really want the fuss of a sleepover.

"I don't think tonight is really appropriate, maybe another night?"

India shook her head but didn't object anymore.

"I thought you'd be up for it, Luce," she muttered. "We *always* had sleepovers."

Everyone gave Lucinda a hug before Trey showed them to the door.

'Why do people keep suggesting things that I'm supposed to like?' thought Lucinda, frowning. 'First, I find a wardrobe full of clothes that I'm supposed to like, but I actually find boring; then Trey states that I like pancakes for breakfast, but I found them too sickly; then India states that I loved sleepovers and we always had them before I got amnesia, and I don't feel that I like them that much. What's happening?'

Lucinda pondered over it a little more, but then shook the worrying thought from her mind.

'Don't be silly,' she scolded herself, 'it's only because you're not yourself. In a few days, you'll be back to your old self. Today's been a big day. You've just discovered you've woken up from a coma! Come on, you're bound to not feel up to fun things like sleepovers and feel a little sick.'

"Hey, your favourite show is on TV," called Trey from the living room. "The Suite Life of Zack and Cody."

Lucinda smiled. Maybe this would be something that she liked. But ten minutes into the show and Lucinda started yawning. She had nothing against the two cute boys, Cole and Dylan Sprouse, but like everything else she had found that day, they were too cute, too sickly, too *sweet*. So sickly sweet. Lucinda's lids started to close and she drifted off into a deep sleep, just like the one she had gone into a year ago.

Chapter 3

Lucinda fiddled with her school tie. It had been three weeks since she had woke up from her coma. Trey had showed her pictures of her when she was younger, pointing out certain events and telling her what had happened, showing her each room in the house and telling her what had happened in them over the years. Lucinda had pointed out a certain room and Trey had opened it for her. But much to Lucinda's disappointment, it was empty. So dark and empty. The other rooms in the house were so bright and happy, but this room looked like one of those old dungeons you found in the Tower of London and the labyrinth underneath Windsor Castle. So cold and dark, an atmosphere of sadness and insanity, a feeling that tortured souls had stayed and died in that room. The walls were painted black, the windows were covered with newspaper, a naked flickering bulb dangled from the ceiling. Despite the room being so cold and empty, Lucinda felt drawn to it,

30

like there was something magnetic in the walls that drew in sweet innocent teenage girls.

"What was this room used for?" she asked, looking around the dimly lit room.

"It was just a junk room. Full of your old toys and old stuff that wasn't worth keeping. After you went to sleep..."

That's how Trey referred to the accident on the cliffs, the amnesia and coma. Lucinda had just gone to sleep. She had just gone into a deep sleep. It made Lucinda sound like Sleeping Beauty or Snow White. In a deep sleep, awaiting true love's first kiss to wake her up again.

"...I thought I should just empty it. If you were here when I had emptied it, you would have cried, 'No, don't chuck that away! Don't get rid of that!'"

Lucinda chuckled, but then turned serious again.

"Did you get rid of things because of mum and dad as well?"

Trey lowered his eyes to the floor and nodded weakly.

Her friends from school had come round every day to check that she was okay and suggested going to see a film on the weekends. Lucinda had nodded, but they had never bothered. Now, it was time for Lucinda to go to school. Her school uniform was as plain and boring as her wardrobe. A biscuit coloured blazer with matching trousers and a plain white top. Slipping on her beige brogues, (She couldn't stand the things, yet there seemed to be at least five pairs of them in her wardrobe.) she looked into the full-view mirror. She did not feel right in the clothes that she wore. At first, she thought it was only because she was not feeling herself, but as the weeks passed, she realized she still felt the same way she did about the things around her and what Lucinda 'liked.' Not that she told Trey that. She thought about changing her uniform. Not entirely, just a few alterations, but she knew that that was against the school rules. Besides, there was nothing bright and bold enough that she owned that would jazz it up a bit. She sighed and trudged downstairs.

"Ready for school?" asked Trey, smiling.

Lucinda smiled bravely and Trey nodded understandably.

"Are we taking the car?" asked Lucinda

"What car?"

"Your car."

"I have no car remember? It crashed."

"Oh. Right. Yeah, I remember."

So they walked to Burns High School, Trey limping with his bad leg, leaning on his crutch for support.

At school, all the teenagers stopped and stared at Lucinda as if she was a ghost.

'They're not looking at me,' she thought, lowering her head. 'They're looking at Trey. Who wouldn't? He looks like someone got Justin Bieber's DNA and mixed it with Zac Efron's to get him.'

But she couldn't escape the fact that they *were* looking at her. She *was* a ghost from the past, now that she was awake. The handsome prince had come and given the princess the kiss of life.

'What kissed me?' shuddered Lucinda. 'What gave me the kiss of life? Why am I alive? What spared me from death? Didn't Trey say that a fall from the cliffs was fatal? Why was I spared? Did Fate and Destiny give me the kiss of life? But why? I was in that coma for a year, why now?'

It was natural curiosity, but Lucinda could not help but wonder. Something was just not quite right. An important piece of the puzzle was missing.

Her friends met her inside and were her map for the day, pointing out different rooms and classes, introducing her to all the teachers. Lucinda felt uncomfortable in everyone's presence. She couldn't shrug off all the eyes that were staring at her, studying her, like she was some unknown specimen.

At the end of the day, she had never felt so eager to go up to her sickly sweet room. But as she was locking her locker, turning away from the laughing teenagers and heading toward the exit, she saw a girl. The girl looked around her age; she had long honey coloured hair with cold blue eyes, like the Antarctic Ocean. She was standing near the exit, clutching her books to her chest, and she was glaring at Lucinda. Lucinda felt a tingle down her spine. The coldness of those eyes, the sheer hate. The hall was no longer a busy, noisy, warm place, but a bitter, cold, and icy place.

"Hey Luce! We were all worried about you! We thought you'd already gone without us!" cried Helen, touching Lucinda's shoulder.

Lucinda hardly heard her, she was so lost into the snowy blizzard of the girl's eyes.

"What's the matter?" asked Helen.

"Who's that?" she murmured, nodding at the girl.

Helen looked and blinked.

"Oh, that's just Joyce Offey. Don't worry about her, she's crazy Lucinda. She's never liked you, but don't worry about it, she isn't violent; she won't hurt you."

"Why doesn't she like me?"

Helen stiffened, then shrugged.

"Just one of those things. You haven't done anything wrong."

Lucinda nodded.

"Come on," beckoned Helen, taking hold of Lucinda's arm. "We'll go out this way. The others are waiting."

Lucinda nodded again, but before she was dragged out of the school, she took one more look at Joyce Offey. She was still there; she hadn't moved a muscle and she was still glaring. Lucinda found herself shuddering again, but then she turned her back on her to join her friends.

Chapter 4

"Enjoy your first day of school?" said a grinning Trey when she got in.

Lucinda nodded vaguely.

"Not so good?" Trey said sympathetically.

Lucinda shrugged. "It was alright I suppose, but I just didn't feel...right...there."

Trey nodded. "I understand, Luce. Don't worry, you'll feel like it's your second home once you get settled. It always was in the past. You loved studying in the school library with your friends after it ended. I suppose it didn't bring back any memories?"

Lucinda shook her head.

"I think I'll go up to my room now," she said, after a pause.

"What about dinner?"

"Erm...why don't you choose for both of us?"

Trey nodded and Lucinda started up the stairs, the cream walls covered in baby photos of Trey and herself.

Lucinda stroked each with her finger, as if the touch would bring back the past she had forgotten.

She entered her bedroom and looked round it for the umpteenth time. She still didn't feel like this was *her* bedroom. It wasn't *hers.* She sighed to herself and flopped onto the bed, wondering what to do. Trey and her friends had mentioned that she had liked studying in the past, so she tried to do a bit of English homework, but she grew bored after only a little while. Trey and her friends were wrong again. But perhaps they weren't? After all, it was Lucinda that had lost her memory. But surely that didn't cause personal likes and dislikes to change too? She sighed again. What was happening to her? What was happening to Lucinda Jordan? Her thoughts then wandered to think about Joyce Offey. The cold, hating girl she had seen standing at the bottom of the hallway at school. According to Helen, Joyce was just a crazy teen that hadn't really taken a shine to Lucinda. But why? Surely there must be a reason. You couldn't look at someone with such icy bitterness just because you didn't like the look of them. There had to be a reason. Lucinda's thoughts of Joyce were cut short as the phone rang and she jumped. Lucinda stared at it for a moment. She couldn't remember seeing a phone in her room, but she shrugged and picked up the receiver.

"Hello?"

There came heavy breathing from the other end.

"Hello?" she called again.

"Lucinda," the person on the other end breathed. Lucinda shuddered. The voice was as cold as Joyce's eyes, whispering the 'c' so long that it sounded like a snake itself had said her name.

"He...hello?" she whimpered, sounding like Callumn.

"Lucinda," it whispered again, then cackled, "Lucinda Jordan."

"Who is this?" demanded Lucinda quietly.

The voice cackled again, "You know me Lucinda. Oh boy, do you know me!"

Lucinda gasped and dropped the receiver onto the floor. Her body was shaking, but she finally found the courage to pick up the receiver again and put it to her ear.

"Who is this?" she whispered, but the person on the other end had hung up. Slowly, she put the phone down and wrapped her arms around herself. She glanced at herself in the mirror. Her eyes were wide, her small body was trembling. She turned her glance away from the mirror and shook her head.

'Don't be scared!' she scolded. 'It was just a prank call. It was probably from Joyce!'

Her thoughts were back on Joyce again and she felt even more scared. Joyce? Calling her? Why? Why had she spoken like that? Lucinda couldn't say she had threatened her because she hadn't, she had just repeated her name in a chilling voice.

'You know me. Boy, do you know me.' Well, of course Lucinda knew Joyce. Well, maybe not so much now seeing as though she has amnesia, but she did before. What had happened between them? It made Lucinda's head ache thinking about it so much. Then Trey called her down for dinner and Lucinda gladly rushed downstairs to get away from the now dark atmosphere of her bedroom.

At dinner, Lucinda dipped her bread roll in her soup absentmindedly, only half-watching Trey spooning tablespoon after tablespoon of soup into his mouth.

"Who is Joyce Offey?" she asked suddenly, making Trey look up from his soup.

"Why? Did you talk to her today at school?"

"No. I just saw her standing near the exit. She didn't look exactly happy to see me. She was sort of...glaring at me."

Trey's tense shoulders sagged as if he was very relieved and he slid his hand over to hers and squeezed it tight.

"Pay no attention to her, Luce. Do you understand? Keep away from her. She means no harm I'm sure, but stay away from her; she's still one of those mean people that's not going to do you any good."

Lucinda nodded and went back to her soup, though now she couldn't sip a drop of it. 'Stay away from Joyce' is what Trey had said. But Trey and Helen had both said that she didn't mean any harm. But if she didn't mean any harm, then who had called her? Or is that not 'harming' in Joyce's books? Lucinda had many questions she wanted to ask about Joyce and what had happened between them, but she held her tongue and forced the soup down her throat.

Chapter 5

A few more days had passed and Lucinda got no more calls from Joyce, but she was still not settling in at Burns High. Her friends asked her how she felt all the time, and sometimes Lucinda got a little annoyed with them and snapped.

"I've told you a million times! I'm not sure yet!"

Her friends jumped at the sudden outbursts and whimpered, "What's got into you, Luce? You never used to shout."

This annoyed Lucinda more because she was always being reminded of what she liked and disliked, when she had already decided she no longer liked it or now loved it. For example, Lucinda was just collecting her chemistry homework and groaned at how hard it looked and how she would never pass the test. India, who was in the same class with her, looked at her in shock and exclaimed, "But Luce, of course you'll pass it! You *love* chemistry!"

Lucinda had frowned and mumbled something like, "Do I?"

As she found, it was actually quite alright, but she didn't *love* it. It was actually the first thing that her friends had got right about her liking something.

Getting ready for school again, she slipped on each boring garment. As she tied her short chocolate hair in pigtails, the phone rang.

"Hello?" she said, picking up the receiver.

There came struggled breathing from the other end; Lucinda stiffened, wondering whether this was another one of Joyce's prank calls.

"Joyce?" she choked out.

There came a raspy chuckle.

"Joyce, stop it! Why do you hate me? What did I do?"

The chuckles stopped and then a voice, different from last time, whispered, "Lusssinda Jordan. Lusssinda Jordan. Lussssinda Jordan."

Lucinda shuddered. This voice was different from last time. It was still a girl's voice, but it was quieter, huskier, more menacing, though the pronunciation of the 'c' was still apparent as an 's.' As if a snake had hissed it.

"Who is this?" whispered Lucinda.

"Samara," it rasped.

"Samara? Is that your name? Do I know you?"

But the person on the other end had hung up.

Lucinda gaped for a moment, holding the receiver in her hand, but then she put it down and sat down on the bed. Samara? Who was she? Did she know Lucinda at school like Joyce? Was she like Joyce and hated her because she just did? Or was it really Joyce, just playing around?

Lucinda was so lost in her thoughts that she nearly didn't hear Trey calling her downstairs so he could walk her to school.

Lucinda jumped downstairs, grabbed her backpack, and was just about to race out of the front door when Trey called, "Hey! Wait for me!"

"Trey, I'm okay; I'm fifteen, not five! I'm sure I'm quite capable of walking to school by myself! It's also not fair on you walking there every day when you have a bad leg."

Trey nodded. "Thanks for your consideration, Luce, but I need to make sure you get to school safely. It's just brotherly concern. I wouldn't want you to get hurt again."

It was Lucinda's turn to nod at Trey's consideration.

"I know, Trey, but I'll be fine...really. It's not like I'll go to the graveyard and jump off the cliff, is it? I mean, I don't even know where the graveyard or the cliff is!"

Trey winced and gave it some thought.

"Alright," he sighed reluctantly. "But be careful, Luce. Promise me."

"I'll be fine, Trey, I promise. There's nothing to worry about, is there?"

Trey blinked and then shook his head.

As Lucinda walked to school, she looked at the streets she passed. When Trey walked with her, she didn't need to pay attention to the surroundings because Trey knew where he was going and he'd lead her to school and then back home, but now that she was walking to school on her own, she had to know where she was going. Instead of hanging her head so that she only looked at the dirt on the path, she looked at and passed all the pretty dollhouse like houses, passed all the other children going to school, passed a graveyard...

Lucinda stopped and stared at the graveyard entrance. There were no gates, so it gave you a proper view of all the tombstones and the flowers that lay beneath them. Despite being a graveyard it looked pretty in the daytime. A peaceful place for the dead, but come night, Lucinda knew it'd be just like the graveyards that you saw in horror films. A foggy and sinister atmosphere where you expected to see the ghosts of the damned wander around, looking for eternal peace.

Lucinda shuddered. Something had definitely happened to her there. Something terrible. Well, of course it was terrible. It made her lose her memory. She didn't even recognise her own face when she peered into the mirror when she first woke up! She then started to really wonder what had gone on that night. What had happened there and how and why she had fallen off that cliff? Where was the cliff around here anyway? Lucinda would've gone in search for the cliff, hoping it would maybe jog her memory as it seemed that nothing else had up to now, but she knew that if she went exploring she'd be late for school. She didn't think that would go down well with the teachers despite her just coming out of a coma and the teachers looking at her like she was some sort of ghost and would be glad for her to be out of their presence. Shaking all morbid thoughts from her head, she continued her way to school.

"Helen," started Lucinda at lunch break, "you said you didn't know what happened on the cliffs the night I lost my memory, but does somebody here?"

Helen looked up at her from biting into her apple.

"Not that I know of."

"What about you, Callumn? Apple? Do you know anyone that would know?"

Apple and Callumn shook their heads, Lucinda thinking they did so a little desperately, so they could get back to talking about *normal* teenage stuff like films, music, and celebrity gossip.

"What about Joyce?"

Everyone on her table jumped.

"Joyce? What would she know about it?"

"I don't know, but a few nights ago, she called me and..." She trailed off, wondering whether she should tell them or not.

"Joyce *called* you?" cried India, looking nervously at Helen and Callumn.

"Well...I think so. I'm not so sure, but I only thought it was her because she..."

"She what?" asked Callumn desperately. "Did...did she...threaten you...or some...something?"

Lucinda shook her head. "No, she just sort of..."

Everyone leaned in, staring at her with anticipation.

"I can't explain it," sighed Lucinda. "It was like she was warning me."

"Warning you of what? What exactly did she say?" asked Apple.

"Well, I don't know. She said, 'You know me.' I mean, I don't know what she meant by that, but she sort of said it in a 'don't mess with me or else' tone."

Helen looked at Callumn, who looked at Apple, who looked at India, who stared at Lucinda.

"What else did she say?" asked Helen.

"Nothing really. She just said my name over and over."

Helen nodded, but she looked... 'What?' thought Lucinda. 'Frightened? Shocked? A look of nothing? Wasn't she surprised that this had happened?' She couldn't see the true feelings or thoughts that were in Helen's heart, nor could she read Apple's deep sea eyes or India's petite and usually emotional face.

Lucinda shivered. Why was it that people seemed to be hiding things from her? She wondered whether to mention the mysterious Samara and the chilling phone call she had had that very morning, but she decided not to. Talking about Joyce Offey was grim enough!

Another day at school had ended and Lucinda opened her locker to take out her coat and homework from previous classes in the day that she had just shoved in. Carefully keeping an eye out for Joyce's cold stare, Lucinda was as quiet as possible as if she was the only one in the hall rooting around in her locker for the things she had to take home that day and if she did make a sound, Joyce would suddenly appear, looking right at her with those cold, unemotional eyes.

Lucinda shut her locker and locked it, shoving the key into a front pocket of her backpack. When she looked up, a gasp caught in her throat as she came nose-to-nose with Joyce Offey! Lucinda widened her eyes but could not find the energy, nor the courage, to do anything else. It felt as though those cold eyes were so cold that they had frozen Lucinda to the spot just by looking into them.

"Enjoying school, *Lucinda,*" she hissed.

"Y...yes," gulped Lucinda, sounding as bad as Callumn.

Joyce smirked. "Strange. You never used to."

"But my friends said I did. They said I always came on top with all the subjects."

Joyce snorted. "You call them *friends*? Though you didn't, did you? Before, I mean. You told me that they were pathetic excuses for humans and said they were weak. You especially hated little Callumn Hanks."

Lucinda shook her head in disbelief. Why would she say anything as cruel as that? India, Apple, Callumn, and Helen were her friends. They came to visit her when she was in a coma, they were happy to see her alive and well again. She couldn't say the same thing for Joyce; well, Trey never mentioned her coming over to see her. But even though she liked her friends, she had no recollection of them whatsoever. Those first hugs hadn't felt right. They had no effect on her. Was it because before she lost her memory, she had hated and loathed them? Secretly hanging out with Joyce and moaning about them, telling her what pitiful excuses for humans they were? No! She would never do that! But she became more and more confused just thinking about it. Did her friends *know* that she hated them and liked the thought of her losing her memory so that they could teach her anew and make her like and dislike the things they wanted her to like and dislike? But why should she believe Joyce? Joyce was crazy, according to Helen and Trey, but then again, why should she believe them...

"I would never say anything like that!" cried Lucinda. "Not about my friends!"

Joyce scoffed, "But you did."

Lucinda gulped. Could Joyce know much more than she was letting on?

"Do you know or did you know anyone here with the name of Samara?" she found herself asking.

Joyce smiled an evil smile.

"Why, didn't you know, Luce? The only Samara that came to this school was a *murderer!*"

She chuckled wickedly, then skipped away as if she had been told that she had a hot date tonight with the most popular boy in school, leaving Lucinda gaping and feeling very, very scared.

Chapter 6

Lucinda shook with fear as she teetered home, thinking about the mysterious Samara. When she came across to the graveyard again, she stared and stared at it. She suddenly gasped, making a couple who were just coming out of the graveyard jump. She nodded at them apologetically and then turned her focus back to the graveyard. What if Samara had actually been on the cliffs with her on the night she lost her memory? Did Samara *push* her off? A million questions started to race through her mind. If Samara had been on the cliffs with her, then where was she now? Was she still alive? Had she been waiting for Lucinda to wake up so she could terrorise her again? But why? How did she find out that Lucinda was still alive? Even Trey said that a fall from the cliff was usually fatal. Samara couldn't possibly be dead; Trey hadn't mentioned that anyone else had been found near the cliffs along with her body, but Joyce made it sound as though Samara was dead. She used past tense when she mentioned Samara going to school. She decided when she got home that she'd ask Trey about it, but maybe that wasn't such a good idea. Like her friends, Lucinda knew that he liked to keep her in the dark from...from what? Lucinda had a feeling he knew much more than he let on about what went on at the cliffs, but why didn't he tell her? She decided not to ask him after all. Maybe if she left matters for a while, he might tell her in time.

Lucinda didn't say a word as she entered her home.

"Luce! Hey! Are you alright? Did you have a good time at school today?" grinned Trey.

Lucinda nodded and trudged straight upstairs. Trey limped out of the living room. He was about to ask her what she wanted for dinner, but all he saw was her feet disappearing up the stairs. He frowned in a puzzled fashion to himself.

'Strange. Lucinda never used to do that. She always stayed downstairs to talk about her day and help with dinner,' he thought, but he merely shrugged and hopped to the kitchen to make dinner.

"You're quiet tonight," remarked Trey at dinner.

Lucinda shrugged.

"Was everything alright at school? Joyce didn't give you any grief, did she?"

He said the name 'Joyce' as if it was a swear word and only whispered it.

Lucinda shook her head and to steer away from the subject of school and Joyce Offey, Lucinda asked about her parents. Trey stiffened as if reluctant to talk about them.

"It was really unfortunate how they died. I told you they died in a car crash and they did, almost crushing my leg, and I told you that you were with your friends watching a film..."

"Why wasn't I with you?"

"They were taking me to college."

"I thought you had your own car."

"That was my car. We shared it. Our parents didn't really drive; they believed in fresh air and exercise and walked a lot, so when I came of age to buy a car, they gave me theirs to save money and space."

"Oh," was all Lucinda could manage. Something about his story didn't add up.

"They were good parents. They were so good to us, Luce; you were devastated when you found out they were dead, then you fell off the cliff..."

He looked like he was near tears, so Lucinda started on another subject.

"Okay, Trey. We'll talk about them later. Look, I need some help with this math homework I got today, would you mind helping me with it? I don't think I entirely understand it."

Trey blinked at her.

"But Lucinda," he said, "you *love* math!"

Chapter 7

Lucinda sighed, frustrated. She *hated* her clothing. There was a limit to how much she could take with all this sickly sweet nonsense. She flung each flimsy blouse and each pastel coloured trouser to the floor, glaring at each one in disgust. She didn't care what Trey said, she did not like this sort of clothing anymore. Today was a Saturday and India had called that morning to ask if she would like to go to the cinemas. Lucinda, desperate to get away from the tiring homework she supposedly loved, agreed, but she couldn't make up her mind as what to wear. At this rate, she wouldn't be going out at all! She sighed again and shoved on a pale pink sweater with light blue jeans. Maybe she could do something with her hair too, but there were only pretty little bows, cream coloured bobbles and butterfly hairclips to put in her hair. She frowned. Like the spare empty room, she'd have to have a clear out in here and go on a major shopping trip. She paused, thinking about that dark, dreary room. She wondered whether it would make a good bedroom. For her of course. The room she was in now bored her. Every ounce of her screamed and demanded change. But she could not think or discuss these matters now with Trey, she had a date with India, Apple, and Callumn. Helen could not go to the cinemas for she was at the dentist and then had to go shopping with her parents.

Opening the front door, she called a quick notice that she was going out with friends to Trey and then left.

"I loved that movie!" exclaimed Lucinda, coming out of the picture house with her friends, finishing off the tub of popcorn.

"I did too," smiled India weakly. "But it's a change from what you usually went for."

Lucinda stopped munching on her popcorn and frowned.

"What do you mean?"

"You usually don't go for things with vampires or werewolves in them," stated India. "Before you went for things that were sweet, touching, and romantic."

Lucinda pretended to yawn—she was sick of pretending to act surprised or sorry about the things she *really* liked.

"Bor-ing. I want something with action."

India and Apple laughed weakly. Callumn didn't say or do anything. He tagged along like he normally did. Lucinda thought of something then. She looked at India and the dark clothes that she was always wearing, completed with her dark make-up.

"Erm...India, I know this is a little cheeky, but could I come round to your house and borrow some of your clothes? I mean, just for a little while. I'm sick of wearing these pale washed-out things!"

India jumped as if Lucinda had *insulted* her clothing.

"Well...yeah. Of course you can."

"Thanks," smiled Lucinda.

But as Lucinda was smiling, India shared a nervous glance at Callumn and Apple, who looked at India with worry.

"Wow!" cried India, as she stared at Lucinda in awe. She couldn't believe how pretty she looked in her clothes. Lucinda had picked a black mini-skirt with a combat top that showed small parts of her stomach. She had also chosen to take home (just in case she wanted to change) a pair of some black drainpipe jeans and a tight black leather top that zipped up at the front and showed a lot of her stomach. Lucinda grinned as she peered into the mirror. She looked so different, so much better, even India agreed that she did and it looked as though Callumn and Apple did too. They gaped at her, their eyes darting from her bare legs to her face (which she had made up with lots of India's heavy make-up) to the parts of her stomach that was exposed. She grinned to herself again. She felt so much better.

Much better than the pretty little girly things back at home.

"I feel so much better," breathed Lucinda.

"You...you look...pretty," said Callumn, managing weak smile, but he didn't sound so sure. In fact, he sounded *afraid*, but Lucinda was too happy and too busy admiring her new look to notice and nodded thanks to him.

"You look just like..."

"Like who?" asked Lucinda turning to him.

"Oh...no one. You don't...really. I...was j...ju...just being silly."

Lucinda looked at him quizzically, but then shrugged.

"I'll give you these back when I've been shopping," promised Lucinda to India.

"Oh, it's alright. Don't worry about it. You can keep them. They were getting too small for me anyway."

"Thanks, India."

"I'm home!" called Lucinda.

"Hey Lu! How was the film?" asked Trey.

"It was great!"

Trey's usual grin fell as he saw what Lucinda was wearing. Lucinda grinned at him.

"Do you like the new look? I went round to India's and asked if I could borrow some clothes because the things I have upstairs..."

She was cut short when Trey very suddenly yelled, "Lucinda!"

Lucinda jumped a mile. Trey had never shouted at her; he had always been full of smiles and optimism.

"Y...yes?"

Trey looked at her coldly for a moment, which made Lucinda shiver, making her remember Joyce's cold stare. But then he turned his face back to normal. He sighed. To himself?

"I like it, Luce. It suits you," he sighed.

Lucinda raised an eyebrow. If he liked it, then why did he yell at her a minute ago?

"Did you get anything to eat?" asked Trey, breaking the short silence.

Lucinda nodded. "We went to a café."

Trey nodded and went into the living room. Lucinda blinked. What had she done that had made Trey yell? Was it because of what she was wearing? He had said that he loved her wearing the clothes that she hated. She peered at the time. It was only six, but she trudged upstairs anyway. She started wondering what Joyce had said to her about her hating her friends before and started to wonder, if she did say horrible things about her friends, what kind of person she was like before? But as much as she wondered, she refused that she had spoken like that about her best friends. For who, really, would be friends with Joyce Offey? She knew she shouldn't judge people by their looks, but one look into her eyes and you could tell that she was a mean person. She thought about the things that her friends and Trey had stated that she liked, but what she no longer did like. She shuddered as a troubling thought slithered into her mind. What if…if she *had* been a mean girl like Joyce (which she had doubts about), what if Trey had seen his chance and put the sickly sweet things in her possession while she had amnesia, so that they would cover up the dark and horrible things? Like when people sprayed perfume and air fresheners to get rid of bad smells in certain rooms. What if she really was, before she got amnesia, just like one of those bad smells?

Lucinda woke up. It was the middle of the night at least. Lucinda shivered, though she didn't know why. Realizing she needed to go to the loo, she got up and started to her bedroom door when her phone rang. Lucinda stared at it. The fairy lights near the mirror provided her with enough light to see the objects in her bedroom.

The phone rang at least five times before she picked it up, wondering who the hell would be calling at this time of night, though she was afraid to think who.

There came struggled breathing from the other line.

"Joyce! Stop it!" hissed Lucinda.

There came a quiet cackle.

"Samara," it rasped.

"Samara? Is that you? Is that your name?"

Nothing. Just breathing.

"Who are you? Are you the same Samara that Joyce was talking about?" hissed Lucinda, but a little louder now.

The person on the other line hung up.

Lucinda sighed. Where was this girl going? Was this really the mysterious Samara that may or may not be dead? Or was it Joyce Offey pulling a terrible prank?

Lucinda sighed, remembered that she needed to go to the loo, and dashed to the bathroom.

After she had been to the toilet and washed her hands, she switched off the bathroom light, yawned and teetered back to her bedroom. But before she could go back into her bright, happy room, she felt a bitter coldness touch her arms. She instantly got goose bumps. She stiffened, too afraid to turn her head and look down the landing. Her eyes were fixed on her bedroom door. She must've stood there for about five minutes, when eventually she found the courage to turn her head ever so s-l-o-w-l-y to the end of the landing. What she saw made her gasp, but she could only manage half a gasp for she choked at the end with fear. A girl was standing in the doorway of the spare room. Lucinda panted, staring at the girl. She looked around Lucinda's age and was wearing a gloomy grey dress that had mud stains galore on it. She had long brown hair that covered half her face. But what made Lucinda choke in fear and astonishment, was what the girl had in her hand. She was gripping a knife. A blood-stained knife. But as terrifying as the girl was and despite all the questions whirling in Lucinda's mind, she found herself tottering up to the mysterious girl, even though every bone in her body told her not to and run back into her safe, sweet bedroom.

Lucinda cocked her head to the side to see if she could see the girl's face, but the wet mop of brown hair hid too much of it.

"Who...who are you?" asked Lucinda bravely.

The girl seemed to smile evilly under her chocolate coloured curtain and disappeared into the spare room's depressing darkness.

Lucinda followed her; stepping into the spare room, she saw the girl huddled in a corner, rocking herself back and forth.

"Who are you? What are you doing here?"

The girl suddenly stood up and faced her, lifting her head up so that her hair brushed off her face. Lucinda's eyes widened and she screamed.

Chapter 8

Lucinda was running. She was running in the graveyard. She had no idea what she was doing there. She held a knife in her hand, but she had no idea what she was holding it for. She ran through the graveyard, running away... But from what? What was she running from? What was she running to? She heard a twig snap ahead of her and without thinking, she headed towards it. Smiling to herself, she ran through the fog to the cliffs. The girl she had seen earlier was standing there. Before the girl could turn around, everything went black.

"Lucinda?" called Trey, shaking Lucinda awake. "What are you doing in here?"

Lucinda groaned as she opened her eyes. There was hardly any light in her bedroom this morning. Then her eyes snapped open. This wasn't her bedroom. This was the spare room!

"What am I doing here?" she asked herself.

Trey shrugged, thinking the question was directed at him.

"Search me. That's what *I'm* asking *you.*"

Lucinda sat up. She was lying on the floor, right in the centre of the room. She put her hand on her head, trying to remember what she was doing and how she got here. She remembered getting up to go to the toilet, but what had happened after that? She had no recollection of going back to bed...in her bedroom anyway. She was certain she had dreamed something that night, but she couldn't remember what. Thinking it wasn't important, she searched her mind for any memory of the night before. She shook with worry because for a moment, she thought she had amnesia. But of course she had amnesia! She remembered meeting Trey that morning and screaming, then he told her that she had amnesia, then she met her friends, India Peterson, Helen Manson, Callumn Hanks, and Apple Ambrose. She sighed with relief. She hadn't got amnesia again. But she frowned, racking her brains for any recollection of last night. She remembered a girl...

She gasped, "Trey! There was someone here last night!"

"What?"

"A girl! She was standing outside this room, then she disappeared and then...and then...I can't remember much more."

"A girl? Here?" asked Trey, going a little pale.

Lucinda nodded.

"Are you sure?"

Lucinda nodded again.

Trey parted his lips as if he were about to say something, but then he decided not to and licked them instead.

"What's wrong?" asked Lucinda, widening her eyes, wondering if Trey had seen her too.

"Nothing," he said, shaking his head. "Come on, it's Sunday today. Let's go downstairs and make your favourite breakfast, eh?"

Lucinda nodded, though she didn't feel like swallowing one bite of those sickly sweet pancakes.

As they made their way downstairs and into the kitchen, Lucinda suggested, "Look, I know those pancakes are my favourite, but I fancy a change. You know what I feel like? Jam and toast."

Trey blinked.

"Jam and toast?"

Lucinda nodded. Trey stared at her for a moment, but then nodded.

"Jam and toast it is."

As he was taking the bread out from the bread bin and the jam from the fridge, he said, his back turned to Lucinda, "So tell me more about that girl you saw. What did she look like? What was she doing?"

"Well...she was doing nothing. She was just standing outside the spare room, looking at me, though I couldn't really see her face."

"How do you mean?"

"She had really long brown hair and it covered half her face."

Trey blinked but then nodded for her to carry on.

"She was wearing a dress and she looked really dirty, like she'd been outside in the pouring rain and rolled in the mud. I guess that's the only description I can give you. I didn't see her face and I couldn't really see anything else with all the mud that covered her." Lucinda didn't dare tell Trey that she was also carrying a knife.

"And that's it? She didn't say or do anything apart from look at you and then disappear?"

"That about sums it all up," nodded Lucinda.

"Then how did you end up falling asleep on the floor in the spare room?"

Lucinda twisted her face in thought, but then shrugged.

"My guess is as good as yours, Trey. I really don't know."

Trey nodded and placed two slices of jam and toast in front of her.

Lucinda shovelled the two slices down hungrily. The jam oozing off the toast made Lucinda slaver. It looked so delicious. She licked her lips. Nothing had ever tasted so good in the mornings.

Trey blinked at the empty plate.

"You ate that pretty fast."

"I was hungry," mumbled Lucinda.

"What are you doing today then?" asked Trey, making conversation.

Lucinda groaned. "Well, what is there for a fifteen year old girl to do on a Sunday afternoon in this town?"

"The mall's open seven days a week. How about going there with India and your friends?"

Lucinda gave it some thought. She had been thinking of doing some major clothes shopping. She smiled at Trey and nodded.

"Thanks, Trey. That's a great idea."

She raced upstairs to get changed into the clothes that she chose at India's the day before and called India, Helen, and Apple to see if they wanted to come with her to the mall. Lucinda didn't bother calling Callumn, seeing as though he were a boy and would naturally hate clothes shopping.

India, Apple, and Helen agreed to meet her there eagerly.

Lucinda smiled and thought of the all things she'd buy at the mall. It would definitely be something better than the sweet little girly things that were in her wardrobe now.

Lucinda, Apple, Helen, and India wandered around the mall, each with eighty dollars in their pockets. India had already bought some more azure eye shadow, navy pinstripe shorts, lavender net gloves, dark purple tights and a black lacy blouse. Helen had bought a green dress that only reached her knees, a girly pink cardigan, a white lace top and black lace gloves. Apple had bought two cute little dresses, one a pale pink and the other a satin baby blue, a key ring with a cute monkey on wearing a girly pink dress, and also a floaty red blouse with a big red rose near the neck. As for Lucinda, she had nearly already spent all of her money. She had bought four black t-shirts, each with different patterns or styles on them, two pairs of black jeans, a blood red sweater and blouse, black lace gloves, evergreen earrings, black lacy earrings, a combat mini-skirt, the same dark purple tights India bought, wet look black leggings, a black studded bow, and three skeleton badges and a skeleton charm bracelet.

"They're a bit different from what you usually wear," commented Helen, pointing at her purchases.

"I like them," shrugged Lucinda.

Helen smiled, Lucinda thought it looked like a relieved smile.

"You're going through your Goth stage."

"What?"

"Goth stage. It's when you start to like and wear dark things, spooky things like skeletons and dark colours," explained Helen.

Lucinda smiled with Helen, though in Helen's eyes Lucinda could detect...fear? But why would Helen be afraid of Lucinda going through her Goth stage?

"They are nice, I must admit. You have taste, Lu," nodded India. "But I must also admit that they really are different from what you usually go for."

"Goth stage, India," smiled Helen. "She's been in those sweet clothes since she was put inside her pram. It's alright to have a change, Luce, but I hope you return to your old ways soon. We love you when you're sweet."

When Lucinda got home, she proudly showed Trey her purchases. Lucinda didn't really know what to expect from Trey. She didn't know whether he'd be angry, sad, or happy about her new style. It wouldn't harm anyone surely? She was just going through her Goth stage. It was only a stage, a stage that was only temporary.

Trey stared at the clothes and accessories, not saying a word, no emotion in his sparkling blue eyes.

Finally, Trey nodded at her and turned away.

"You don't like them, do you?" sighed Lucinda.

"No, of course not. I mean, it's not that I don't like them, it's just..."

"Just what?"

There was a short pause, but then he sighed and waved his hand as to dismiss her.

"Nothing. Go to your room to put them away."

Lucinda stared at him for a moment, but then she too sighed, grabbed her new clothes, and started upstairs. Reaching her bedroom door, she opened it and walked inside, but gasped. It was completely bare! It was a dark dingy room like the spare room. Then she realized this *was* the spare room! But why would she come in here? Why would she mistake this for her bedroom? She had lived here long enough to know where her bedroom was. But it was an easy mistake to make. She shrugged her shoulders, but before she shut the door to go to her real bedroom, she stood in the doorway for a second. Feeling the comfort the bedroom gave her, though it was as dark and spooky as a dungeon. Then she shivered as she remembered that the girl she had seen the night before had stood there, and quickly retreated from the doorway and to her bedroom.

Chapter 9

Lucinda returned to school. She hadn't seen the girl again or had any funny phone calls, and she felt better in herself now that she had jazzed up her school uniform. She knew it was against the rules, but it wasn't like it was a huge transformation. Just a few accessories and a few small changes. She had added some zips to the beige coloured trousers that she had bought from a craft shop and had stuck them in various places so they'd look fashionable. She had added a punk badge to her blazer and had ripped her shirt so that it was just like the black top she had worn the day before. She put on her studded badge and added studs (what she also bought from the craft shop) onto her backpack.

Trey jumped when he saw her come downstairs.

"You'll get into trouble," he warned.

"Oh come on, Trey. It's not like I changed the whole uniform. It's just a few changes, that's all."

Trey shook his head but didn't pester her about it.

She got the same sort of reaction from her friends when she entered school.

"Luce! You can't do that! It's against school rules!" gasped Apple.

Lucinda shrugged. "Rules-shmules."

At lunch, Lucinda sat down with her friends. She laughed with them about normal things like the wacky things that celebs had done and squabbled about which music and fashion was the best this season. Lucinda had never felt more comfortable. She felt comfortable in herself. Now her uniform had been altered, she felt much better, much more confident.

Then she happened to look over at the other end of the cafeteria and see Joyce Offey. She stiffened as her eyes met Joyce's bitter cold ones, but this time Joyce wasn't looking at her with that evil glare that had frozen Lucinda to the spot before. It was much worse than that. Joyce looked at Lucinda's clothes and grinned at her. A grin so evil, like a satisfied sort of evil smile, so frightening that it turned Lucinda's blood to ice.

Lucinda shuddered as she approached Joyce. She was alone and was slowly taking out all her homework and folders. Lucinda shuddered again, she reached out for her things as if her whole body was icy and cold, not just her smile and eyes.

"Joyce," she called, not as loud as she had intended to be.

Joyce turned to her and gave her a mock grin, which made Lucinda shiver again.

"What do you want, *Lucinda?*"

Lucinda winced. She said that just like the haunting voice on the phone.

"Joyce, who is Samara? Please tell me!"

Joyce smiled coldly. "I'm surprised you don't remember her. You were as close to her as anyone."

"What?" cried Lucinda.

"Do your research. That's what you go to school for."

Cackling evilly, she flicked her hair back and stalked off.

India had asked her if she wanted to go to her house for tea that night, but Lucinda made a quick excuse that she had lots of homework to do and then headed to the school library. She searched and searched everywhere for the name Samara, but she could not find one Samara. She grew frustrated. Was Joyce lying to her? She couldn't be. She finally asked the librarian if she had any records of a Samara that had attended the school in the last five years.

The librarian blinked. "We have only ever had one Samara in this school."

"Have you any records of her?"

The librarian nodded and led her to a door that boldly stated that it was private. Unlocking the door, the librarian led her through and pointed to a folder marked J.

Lucinda nodded thanks to the librarian and rushed to pick it up. She opened it up and a few newspaper cuttings fell out.

"Oh," blushed Lucinda, not wanting to look silly in front of someone, but when she looked up, the librarian was gone, the door only open an inch.

Lucinda picked up the newspaper cuttings and peered at them. Then she wished she hadn't. She gasped.

'MURDER AT BURNS HIGH!

On 3rd March 2009, Samara Jordo

(16.12.95) killed her

friends: Anne-Marie Wharton, Marta Jackson,

Lloyd Delman, Noah Gene, Madeline Johnston,

and Caroline Jackson. Though their deaths occurred on the same night, they were all killed in different brutal and savage ways.

Anne-Marie Wharton, Marta Jackson, and
Lloyd
Delman were the first three to be stabbed to
death in Delman's home on Camborne
Lane.
Noah Gene and Madeline Johnston were
both found run over on Blossom Tree Lane.
Police would not have connected their
deaths
to the others because they were killed in a
different manner and Samara was not old
enough
to drive, but Samara admitted that she had
stolen
her brother's car and had killed them while
going to
the Jackson house to murder Caroline,
Marta's
younger sister. Breaking into the house and
murdering

Beth and Tom Jackson, she crept into Caroline's
bedroom and smothered her with her own pillow.
A girl she had attempted to murder back at Delman's
house, had survived from her wounds and had called the police.
Joyce Offey, the girl that had called the police, made a
statement on Samara's actions,
"I have been Samara's friend since we started High
School and I always knew she had an insane streak in her.
The death of my friends has shook me up, but I am not at all
surprised that Samara killed them. This will not be the last you
hear of Samara."

It was lucky that Joyce called the police when she did;
after Samara smothered Caroline, she had planned to
kill another one of her classmates, Callumn Hanks.
Her parents, Alison and Zachariah, promised they
would get all the help that Samara needed and planned
to get her into a mental clinic as quick as they could.'

Lucinda gasped as she read the article. She peered at each victim and eventually at Samara. She gasped again as she saw her picture. It was the same girl she had seen in her house that night. It was Samara! And Samara was going to kill Callumn! What kind of sick fourteen year old was this?! Why would she want to kill an innocent boy like Callumn? She hoped her parents had locked her up in the tightest, smallest room in the nuttiest mental hospital and left her there forever and ever.

She read every newspaper clipping there was in the folder and all she could feel was her mouth hanging open, her heart pounding and her stomach churning. Samara had not only killed her friends but had killed Steven Madge! One of her friends! Helen and the others had mentioned Steven the day she woke up, but had not discussed how he had died. Lucinda wanted to sob when she read that she had also killed her parents and brother too. Lucinda left Samara's profile till last. With trembling fingers, she scanned Samara's profile. Samara Jordor, (strange how the paper missed out the 'r,' but then again, newspapers sometimes did that) born sixteenth December 1995 (the same birthday as her!) lived with her older brother, mother and father on *Honeysuckle Lane, number eighteen!* Lucinda choked. Samara had lived in the same house she had! The whole family had died on the night she got amnesia! She felt that had something to do with the murder of Samara's brother, mother and father, but what? She had to have some connection with them; it was too coincidental that Samara had killed all her family the same night Lucinda lost her memory. What was she trying to do? Was she trying to warn Samara's family? Was she trying to stop Samara? Or was she just one of those people Samara hated and thought it'd be fun to push off a cliff? But why would Samara want to do that? Joyce had said that she had been close to her. But how close? Was she so close to Samara that she saw right through her and tried to stop her plans so Samara had to get rid of her? But how had Samara died? She died on the same night she was pushed off the cliff, so how did Samara die if she was in fact the one who pushed her off? Then, very spookily, as to answer her question, another newspaper clipping fell from the folder. Thinking she couldn't read anything worse than what she already had, Lucinda picked it up and scanned it. She screamed. Samara was found dead with a knife in her hand at the bottom of the cliff.

Chapter 10

The next morning, Lucinda did not feel like getting up to go to school. She felt sick and she was sure she could not face Joyce or her friends. Her friends had known about Samara. Why didn't they tell her? Why hadn't they told her she was there on the cliffs with her that night? Were they telling the truth when they said they didn't know? Lucinda doubted it. Just like Trey. Lucinda bet he didn't want her to know the whole truth either. She didn't want to go to school, but she didn't want to stay home either. She didn't want to see Trey and even though her new bedroom gave her a weird feeling of comfort and home, she did not want to stay in it. What if Samara had stayed in this bedroom?

"Come on sleepy-head," laughed Trey, entering her bedroom. "You're going to be late for school."

"I don't want to go to school. I don't feel well," groaned Lucinda.

"Not well?" Trey limped over and put a hand on Lucinda's forehead.

"You don't have a temperature, but you do look a little pale. How do you feel?"

"Awful. I feel sick."

Trey nodded. "Well...okay. You can get away with skipping school today, Lu, but if I find out you've been okay all along, you're in for it!"

He laughed to show he was joking, but Lucinda did not laugh with him. She did not even smile.

"Just leave me alone," muttered Lucinda.

Flicking through a family album, Lucinda started to feel a little better. Smiling at the pictures that showed fun times, making up things in her head that could've gone off on that day, it gave Lucinda a lot of comfort. One of the photos was an old black and white photo. There were two children in the picture; one was a curly blonde haired girl with a massive bow in her hair and wearing a girly school uniform. She was beaming from ear to ear. The other child was a boy. He had dark hair in a side-part and was wearing a stricter looking uniform, and unlike the girl, he was scowling because the girl had her arm around him and like any other boy, he did not like being touchy-feely with girls. Lucinda looked at the back. It said Alic Riley and Zach Jord. The picture was so old that some of the words had faded on the back. But Lucinda was bright enough to realize that this was her mother and father when they were very young children and that her mother's name was Alice and the 'Jord' was actually Jordan. Lucinda smiled and flicked over the page, then stopped and gaped. It was a picture of her, but someone else was in it with her. Samara. Lucinda was smiling sweetly at the camera while Samara kept a straight face, her arms folded, her bedraggled hair covering most of her face. The picture had obviously been taken outside Burns High. Lucinda turned the page quickly. She really had been friends with Samara, just like Joyce had said. But what would a sweet girl like her be doing with an evil murderer like Samara?

She shook her head as if trying to erase Samara from her memory. Maybe that's why Lucinda got amnesia. Because remembering Samara after what she had done was too much to handle. She flicked through the photo album, noticing most of the pictures had been torn to leave the background unrecognisable and disfigured, some had just been torn in half. When she reached the end, shutting it, she gave a deep sigh and put it on her bedside table.

She actually felt quite sleepy, despite it being before noon. She rested her head on the pillow and slowly closed her eyes.

Lucinda opened her eyes. It was dark, thundering and raining. She thought she heard a noise from outside. Getting up, she switched on her bedroom light and wrapped her dressing gown around her. But before she opened her bedroom door, she felt a chill go down her spine. What had she done now? She opened the door quickly and screamed. Zachariah lay dead on the landing. It would have looked like he was sleeping, except that there was one give away. His shirt was blood-stained. Lucinda breathed in and out, trying to calm herself, but then she screamed and Samara started toward her, a blood-stained knife tightly held in her hand.

Lucinda woke up screaming. When she had stopped, she realized that it had all been a dream. She expected Trey to come rushing upstairs to see if she was alright, but he didn't. Her stomach grumbled and she realized she was hungry. Sighing, Lucinda got up and started downstairs.

"Trey?" she called when she didn't hear the tapping of Trey's crutch or the blurred voices on TV.

She entered the kitchen and found a banana sandwich, a glass of cola, and a note on the counter waiting for her. She opened the note. It said,

'Saw you were asleep, have just gone out to get some shopping, left some dinner for you just in case you get hungry. Won't be long. Love, Trey.'

Lucinda sighed. Trey shouldn't go out to get shopping with his bad leg, but Lucinda tucked into the sandwich and drink all the same, wondering when he'd be back. She decided to cut her sandwich in half and went to get a knife. Taking the bread knife, she noticed that one knife was missing from the set. She raised her eyebrow but then she shrugged and cut her banana sandwich in half. Although she tried to brush the unease off her shoulders, she couldn't help the feeling of being watched. She put it all to her imagination, put it all down to knowing that Samara the murderer had lived in that house before her. But if Samara was the same age as her (well, would've been) and Trey and her parents had known about her and where she had lived, then why did they decide to move into there? She shuddered as she thought it and didn't dare think that the bedroom she was sleeping in now had been Samara's before. It was bad enough sleeping in a dead person's room, but a dead murderer's bedroom? That was far worse! Lucinda gulped down her sandwich. Then she started to think about her dream. This was the second dream that had something to do with the night of her memory loss. Maybe her memory was slowly coming back in her dreams. She shuddered. In a way she wanted to remember because she wanted to understand, but in a way she didn't. She feared remembering because she knew if she did get her memory back, she'd find out something that she wished she hadn't.

She thought about her life before the accident. Her parents had died in a car crash; her brother had crushed his leg in the same crash; her friend, Steven Madge had been murdered by Samara, and Lucinda had obviously been some sort of friend to Samara, found out she had murdered her parents and her brother, then she had probably threatened Samara with the police and in doing so, she got pushed off a cliff and suffered with memory loss. But how did Samara end up falling off the cliff as well? Trey hadn't mentioned anyone else falling with her. Why would he keep that secret away from her? Was there a struggle? Did Samara feel guilty killing one of her best friends so she threw herself off the cliff as well? Impossible. If Samara killed six of her best friends and attempted to kill another one of her best friends, one more wouldn't matter to her. Then when Samara and her parents had died, her family had moved into the very same house she used to live in? Lucinda shook her head. No! She refused to believe Samara had lived in the same house as she was living in now. There must have been a mix-up with the streets or the numbers. It might've been a Honeysuckle Road she had lived on or Honeysuckle Street, maybe they got the street name wrong and it was something like Honeycomb or just Honey. Lucinda doubted that there was more than one street called Honeysuckle, or anything else to do with honey for that matter, but they could've always mixed up the numbers. Maybe Samara had lived down the road or next door, but even that thought was troubling to Lucinda.

It actually scared Lucinda how much in common she had with Samara. Samara's parents were dead, so were hers. Lucinda's brother wasn't dead, but he was injured, maybe permanently, and from what she's seen of her bedroom and what Samara wore in her pictures, she had the same sort of style Lucinda has now, but surely that was purely coincidental; Lucinda was only going through her Goth stage, it wasn't as if it was permanent. Suddenly, a horrible thought occurred to her. It made her want to cry out and sob. Since she had woken from her long, fairy tale princess-like sleep, she had encountered strange dreams, strange behaviour from her friends and her brother, she knew secrets were being mysteriously and deliberately kept from her, and she had had strange phone calls that were maybe or maybe not from Joyce Offey. Why was she not living happily ever after like the princes and princesses after the magic true love's kiss in fairy tales?

But she had seen Samara, she was with her all the time. She could feel it. She could feel Samara's cold eyes on her, almost as cold as Joyce's, as she lived her life and saw her friends. She was appearing to her in dreams. What if Samara was trying to take over her? What if Samara made sure that Lucinda does die, even in death? It made Lucinda's heart beat like a drum. She was developing Samara's love of dark clothes and dark things like the bedroom. Maybe that really was Samara's bedroom before and her family knowing it was just used it as a junk room. As much as Lucinda tried, she could not get over her parents buying the house that had belonged to a teenage murderer. What must have the Lucinda she had left behind on the cliffs thought about it? Knowing she was going to live in the same house as her friend and the girl that had tried to murder her? She can't have liked the idea…she still doesn't! But shaking her head again, shaking all the thoughts of

Samara living in her house and convincing herself the profile paper had made a mistake, she put the plate and the glass in the sink and washed them, wanting company more than ever.

Chapter 11

When Trey returned from the shops a while later, Lucinda jumped out into the hall and flung her arms around him.

"Hey, hey!" cried Trey, "What's with all the sudden affection?"

"I love you, Trey. You're the best brother in the world. Don't go to the shops without me again, whether I'm asleep or not."

Trey laughed. "You got it."

He hopped to the kitchen and emptied his bag of groceries on the counter.

"Let me help you," offered Lucinda.

Trey smiled and Lucinda began grabbing all the jars and putting them in the right cupboard.

"Were you alright without me?" asked Trey.

Lucinda nodded. "But just don't leave me on my own again, okay?"

Trey chuckled. "Sure thing, sis."

Lucinda smiled and put away the food.

Apple called that evening and asked if Lucinda wanted to go out with their friends to McDonalds. Lucinda eagerly said yes. She had not wanted to go to school because there were too many people, but her group of friends was small and easier to be in and it was easier to relax; besides, she really needed company right now.

Getting ready, she put all her new clothes up to her, wondering which top to wear and what she'd wear with it, but remembering her thoughts earlier about Samara wanting to take over her body, she shook her head and put all her dark clothes down. Deciding to fight it, she slipped on the clothes she had loathed before. She slipped on some powder blue trousers with a white camisole. She could always put on her knitted baby blue cardigan with the white flower embroidered on the pocket if she got chilly. She looked at herself in the mirror, and for the first time since she woke up from her coma, she did feel like herself. She felt like Lucinda Jordan. She stroked her hair that had grown almost to her shoulders since she woke up.

'Hmm,' she thought, 'a haircut and I'll be me again.'

She smiled as she stepped downstairs, feeling so much better and fresher.

'Funny,' she thought, 'how much gentle colours can do to your feelings. To make you feel calmer and fresher.'

She called out to Trey that she was meeting her friends again, adding that she loved him (that was what the old Lucinda would've done) and she walked out.

Lucinda grinned happily as she saw her friends waiting for her outside of McDonalds.

"Hey! You've come out of your Goth stage! That was a quick stage!" smiled Helen.

Lucinda laughed and tossed her hair back. "Who says the stage's over?"

She laughed, but then thinking that's not what the old Lucinda would've said, she quickly said, "Of course it's over. I don't want to see those morbid garments again. Funny what you do when you're a teenager, huh?"

Helen laughed and they entered McDonalds. Thankfully, the restaurant wasn't very busy, just a few more groups of friends that had decided to go out for a bite to eat. They seated themselves in a corner and one by one, they ordered what they wanted. Lucinda was tempted to order a hamburger with fries and a coke, but knowing that that wasn't what the real Lucinda would order, she ordered a vanilla milkshake, small fries, and a butterscotch ice-cream. She hated sickly tastes like butterscotch but it's what the old Lucinda would've liked, so she force-fed herself, pushing spoonful after spoonful of the sickly sweet, creamy substance into her mouth, slurping the vanilla milkshake, trying not to gag, laughing with her friends about celeb gossip and TV shows, just like the old Lucinda would've done.

But the happy atmosphere turned cold when the Ice Queen herself walked in. Joyce Offey sauntered into McDonalds, her eye catching Lucinda. She smirked at her as she glided to the counter and ordered a hamburger with fries. Lucinda shuddered. She was so thankful she hadn't ordered that.

"Well, look at who we have here," smirked Joyce, strutting up to the small group. She spied Lucinda's order and waved her order in her face.

"Get that away from me," frowned Lucinda, batting the bag of burger and fries away from her face.

"But you love it, *Luce*! This is your favourite thing to have at McDonalds."

"No it isn't, Joyce," frowned Callumn. "She...she ordered what...she orders all the...the time...when she...she comes here. Butter...butterscotch ice-cream and...and fries with...vanilla shake."

"Bu...butt...butter...butterscotch...ice-cream," mocked Joyce, sipping from her coke and laughing.

"Leave him alone, Joyce," India warned, her voice turning cold and hard.

"Or you'll do what? Pour sickly sweet butterscotch ice-cream down my throat to turn me into what you've turned *her?*" she laughed, pointing at Lucinda. "Whatever!"

"What do you mean what they've turned me into?" asked Lucinda, raising an eyebrow.

"Oh just ignore her, Lu," interrupted India, putting an arm around her shoulder, "She's crazy. Ever since..."

India paused and glanced at Joyce, expecting her to say something.

"Yeah, you can say it! Everyone thinks I went crazy the night..." Joyce started.

"Samara killed your friends and tried to kill you too," finished Lucinda.

Everyone gaped at Lucinda.

108

"You've got some of your memory back then?" smiled Joyce evilly.

Lucinda shook her head. "No, I read about it."

"Where?" gasped Apple.

"I sort of looked for a Samara in our school records and found all these newspaper clippings of her and her murders."

Joyce snickered. "Killed your precious Steven Madge and she would've done precious little Callumn Hanks if I hadn't stopped her."

"Yes, you called the police, didn't you? But you hate Callumn and you're as cold and as twisted as Samara, so why did you tell on her?"

"I didn't say *I* hated Callumn, I said you did! And I am not like her! Look in the mirror and take a look at yourself, will you? *And* if I hadn't stopped her, she would've killed the whole town, then she would've moved on to another town and then another, making each one extinct. Did you want that to happen?"

Lucinda shook her head. "And what do you mean 'look at myself in the mirror?' Do I look like Samara to you?"

Joyce smiled evilly.

"Is that why you waved the burger in my face? Because it was Samara's favourite? I'm not Samara, Joyce!"

Joyce snickered.

"You'll find out everything soon, Lucinda Jordan. Soon, you'll know the truth and then you'll get your memory back!"

With that, she turned on her heel and headed to the opposite corner of the restaurant.

"What else did she say to you about Samara?" asked India, biting on her lower lip.

"It's a long story. But when I found out about her, I started seeing Samara, I started having dreams. Oh god, India! I think she's trying to take over my body so she can live again! That's why I'm wearing my old things again, because those dark things are the sort of things she would've worn, wasn't it?"

Her face crumpled, she wanted to sob, but her friends stared at her wide-eyed.

"Have you told Trey about this?" asked Apple.

Lucinda sniffed and shook her head.

"Then you should tell him. Go home now, Luce. Tell him everything. I'll walk you home."

Lucinda shook her head. "No, it's okay, really. I'll be fine walking on my own."

Without waiting for an answer or protest, she got up and ran from McDonalds and all the way home. The one that had supposedly belonged to a murderer.

When she got home, Trey was sat in front of the TV watching some game show. He smiled as Lucinda entered the living room.

"Hey little sis, did you have a nice time? Luce? What's wrong?"

"Trey, I need to talk to you. Please listen to me."

"Luce! What's wrong?"

Lucinda started sobbing; Trey started to get up to embrace her, but Lucinda rushed upstairs to her room.

After half an hour, she had calmed down and she started to slip into her pyjamas. Before she put on her pyjama top however, she noticed a scar across her stomach. She looked in the mirror and stroked it. It was quite big and deep; it surprised her that she hadn't noticed it before. She started to wonder where it came from, but knowing she had to talk to Trey about Samara, she shrugged and put on her top.

"Trey," she breathed, entering the living room again.

"Luce? Oh Luce, are you alright? Whatever got you in such a state when you first came in?"

"Listen to me, Trey. I'm going to tell you something and I want the truth; I don't want any more lies, cover-ups or secrets. I want you tell me everything that I have to know."

She took a deep breath before continuing.

"Joyce told me about Samara. She said she was a murderer and just left me wondering about her. I started getting phone calls, started to have dreams, like flashbacks of what really happened on the cliffs. That girl I told you I saw that night, it was Samara Jordo. She went into the spare room and I followed her in, then...I just can't remember, but she had been there that night. It had been her! She was holding a knife in her hand. Then when I couldn't take it anymore, I went to see if I could find her in the school records and found lots of newspaper clippings on those she had killed. She liked dark things, Trey, and as you know I've recently developed a taste for dark things. She used to live in this house, Trey. She used to sleep in my *room*. She murdered her parents here. I think I was her friend and that I tried to stop her

113

murdering and in doing so, she pushed me off the cliff. Trey, I think Samara's trying to take over me. I think she wants to take over me so she can live again."

She looked at Trey's face. He was as pale as a ghost. As pale as a *corpse*.

"Then you know the truth," he breathed.

"What truth?" cried Lucinda, "I'm no closer to finding out the truth than your leg getting better anytime soon!"

Trey sighed, staring at her shoulder length brown hair and her scared face.

"Lucinda, don't you see? Samara wasn't just your friend. No! That's not the right way to put it. Lucinda, listen... You are not Lucinda Jordan. You are Samara! You are Samara Jordan!"

Chapter 12

"What?" cried Lucinda. "How can I be Samara? We're not even related! I..."

"Lucinda was your twin sister, Samara," sighed Trey.

"What? How can that be? Samara's parents were called Alison and Zachariah, my parents were called *Alice* and *Zach*! I even saw it on the back of that picture that was taken when they were kids! And how come Samara's name said 'Jordo' instead of Jordan?"

Trey shook his head. "No. Some of the words have rubbed off and now the 's' in Alison looks like a 'c' and 'ariah' has rubbed off too. That's probably what happened to our last name to make it look like Jordo, or someone got it wrong. No, you are not Lucinda, Samara."

"They can't be the same! Our parents died in a car crash!"

Trey shook his head. "That was a lie. I told you that to protect you, so you wouldn't remember Samara. The spare room was her room. It was so dark and depressing and when you woke up I didn't want you to know you had a twin sister. I thought we'd be happier forgetting her. But I guess it was only a matter of time before you found out about her or remembered her. Samara," he breathed.

"Stop saying I'm Samara, Trey! I'm not Samara! This isn't funny!"

"Yes, you are! I just thought that you weren't feeling yourself when you refused the things that Lucinda used to like, but then you started dressing like Samara, acting like her, liking the things she liked. I thought she was taking over you just like you did, but then I realized that you *were* Samara, that Lucinda *did* die on the cliff that night. I realized that Lucinda was coming back to tell you who you really are, making you dress like you used to, liking the things that you used to so you'd realize who you were again."

116

"No! No, I won't listen! I'm not Samara!" screamed Lucinda, but who was not Lucinda.

"Lucinda was found with a knife in her hand, that's why I thought she was Samara, but then...Joyce..."

"Joyce? What did Joyce tell you?"

"She told me she was there. She saw you two struggling with each other and you pushing Lucinda off the cliff, she said that Lucinda stabbed you before you pushed her."

Lucinda slid up her pyjama top. The scar was there. The scar that the real Lucinda gave her, and quite rightfully too.

Trey nodded at it. "You are Samara. Don't you remember, Samara? Don't you remember killing your best friends that night at the party? Nearly killing Joyce, but only she survived? Do you remember staying at a mental hospital for half a year? Do you remember killing Lucinda's friend Steven Madge? Do you remember stabbing Callumn in his neck, robbing him of his normal speech? It's a miracle he survived."

Lucinda/Samara shook her head, running her hands through her hair.

"I can't be Samara!" she cried. "I am Lucinda Jordan! We don't even have the same hairstyle! Samara had long hair whereas I had short."

"That's another reason why I thought you were Lucinda. I told you I was at college most of that year. You must've swapped haircuts while I was away. Samara hated anything that you liked, wore, or did, but if she could confuse people and mock you in front of people, then she'd mimic you all she could. Oh Samara, can't you remember? Can't you remember poisoning your mother and then stabbing your father right in front of Lucinda's eyes? Can't you remember chasing her to the graveyard and then to the cliffs? Can't you remember the night before you got amnesia, you meddled with my car so the brake wouldn't work, making me crash it and crush my leg?"

"No!" she screamed, now sobbing and backing off into the corner of the living room. She refused to believe that she was Samara. Refused to believe that it was her that had murdered her friends, Steven Madge, and had attempted to kill Lucinda's friends too. She refused to believe that she was evil and twisted enough to be Joyce Offey's friend, to kill her mother and father and attempt to kill her own brother. To kill Trey. No! She would never do that! But it explained so much. Trey had wanted to keep Samara a secret, to forget her forever, so he had ripped the pieces of each picture off where she was. It explained why a knife was missing in the knife set in the kitchen. It explained why she wanted dark things; it explained why Trey and her friends wanted to keep things from her, why Joyce acted so coldly to her. The girl she had seen in the spare room that night wasn't Samara, but Lucinda. She remembered. She remembered she had cut her hair so she would see what Lucinda would look like with her hair, knowing she'd grow it because she didn't want to look totally identical to her. She loved the way Lucinda and her parents flinched when she came too close. She had loathed India and Helen because they thought they knew it all; she loathed Apple because all she was, was a spoilt daddy's girl; she loathed Callumn and Steven because they were wimpy brats, and she especially loathed her twin sister, Lucinda because she was a goody-two-shoes who was so sickly sweet she'd make anyone vomit just looking at her. She had only tagged along with Joyce, Caroline, Noah, and the rest because they hated Lucinda's group of friends too. She had killed all her friends, laughing in their faces as they gasped their last breaths. She remembered cutting the wire for Trey's car brake and had giggled mercilessly when she watched him speed off with it. Poor Trey, he had only come back home from college a day ago and now he would never return home again. She remembered slipping rat poison into her mother's tea. Her mother had refused to drink it, knowing that it was Samara who had made it. She refused it, knowing Samara wouldn't make anyone a cup of tea without good reason. So Samara had to forced it down her throat, which was good fun because she loved to see her mother struggle. She laughed as she watched her mother die, but her father wasn't laughing. He had seen everything. When he gagged and asked what the hell she was doing, she had turned on him and grabbed the biggest knife she could get from her kitchen. She had chased her father upstairs and stabbed him, just to see Lucinda come out of her bedroom. Lucinda screamed and Samara laughed, turning on her too. Lucinda threw something at her, but it missed. Samara chuckled at Lucinda's weakness and stupidity but only to find that she tripped on it instead. Seeing her chance, Lucinda scrambled outside and ran. Ran anywhere. Anywhere where Samara wouldn't find her, but she did. Samara grumbled but got up quickly and ran after Lucinda, knife in hand. On the cliffs, they had struggled, Samara had dropped the knife somewhere and Lucinda had picked it up and now was using it to scare Samara away. But Samara was not so easily scared off. Lucinda was there. At the foot of a cliff. One good push and she would be gone. She remembered Lucinda stabbing her and then she was pushed to her death. Before Samara fell with her, she had seen Joyce glaring at her from the cemetery gates, and she heard Trey's car crash and Trey calling for his sisters.

Now, as Lucinda who was not Lucinda but Samara, she felt angry again. She wanted to *kill*. She grabbed the lamp off the coffee table she was near to and swung it at Trey's head. Trey's head was not hard to miss for he was at her level, hoping to sooth and comfort her. She was sat down in the corner and Trey was on the balls of his feet to get to her level. It hit his head hard and he fell, groaning. Samara raced to the kitchen and grabbed a knife from the set. It was obvious she had used the missing knife to kill her father and what she had been killed with and that had laid with Lucinda, but this one she was using now was sharp enough. She raced out of the house, Trey gasping and scrambling to his feet, called, "Samara! No!"

But Samara wasn't listening. She went straight on, not knowing where she was going, just going where her feet took her.

She bumped into Joyce, who did not seem so surprised to see her.

"Samara?" she smirked.

Samara grinned, lifting the knife so Joyce could see it.

"Time to finish what we started two years ago, Joyce," she smiled evilly, her voice as rough as gravel.

Joyce smiled evilly with her.

"And what are we going to do, Samara? Where are we going first? India Peterson? Callumn Hanks?"

Samara shook her head.

"Why am I bothered about those lowlifes? I mean *us*. I didn't finish my task in Lloyd's house, did I?"

Joyce gaped and then closed her mouth again, not wanting to show fear.

"And what are you going to do, Samara Jordan? Push me off a cliff like you did your poor, sickly sweet twin sister?"

Samara continued to have that evil smile pasted on her face.

"Maybe," she said, mysteriously. "I may have other plans for you, Joyce Offey."

She cackled as she grabbed Joyce's arm and pulled her towards her. Joyce thought she was going to drag her to the cemetery or the cliffs, but she gasped as she felt something sharp pierce her skin. She looked down. The knife Samara was holding was now pressed into her stomach.

"Oh Samara," she gasped. "I always knew I'd die at your hand. We both knew, right from the moment you opened your eyes from the coma, that you'd remember who you really were someday."

Samara snickered and let Joyce fall to the ground, letting her gasp her last breaths. Samara stared at her. Her cold eyes turned colder, for now there was no light of life in them. Then Samara suddenly noticed that it had started to rain. Her shoulder length hair was already plastered to her face and Joyce's long blonde hair looked as though it was melting into the street. Samara turned her head away from Joyce's body and spotted Trey limping toward her.

He saw Joyce's body and gasped. He did not feel sad about Joyce's death, he had never liked Joyce and he knew she was as twisted as her dead friends, but he was gasping in fear. Samara had really come back.

He limped away and Samara laughed cruelly. Trey shuddered, his back was turned but he could still see Samara's taunting and mocking glare, her eyes that sparkled with insanity. He hopped wherever he could. Pausing for a breath, wondering if Samara was still behind him, but when he checked to see who was behind him, he saw no one. Trey sighed with relief and looked at the place where he had limped to. He had gone into the cemetery! He could see the cliffs not so far away. He gasped and stumbled, nearly falling into a newly dug grave.

"Whoa!" he breathed. Grabbing his crutch, he started out of the cemetery. He had to find Samara. Samara may be a murderer and kill him as soon as see him, but she was his sister and she needed help. *Professional* help. Just like she did when she killed her friends.

But he did not need to look far, Samara was stood at the gates of the cemetery, grasping her knife, a smug and cruel smile pasted on her face.

"Samara," started Trey.

Samara did not listen, she strode towards him, not saying a word. Her face said it all.

"Samara, no! Stop!"

But when he realized that Samara was not going to pay any attention to him, he started to hop away on his crutch as fast as he could. But where could he go? The graveyard had no cover apart from mausoleums and they would be locked. He had nowhere to run, nowhere to hide. He had to go to the cliff. They had to finish what Samara had started.

Heading towards the cliff, he spotted three newly dug graves in a row. Trey shuddered.

'One for Joyce, one for Samara, and one for me,' he thought.

When he reached the cliff, he turned to face Samara.

"Samara! Please stop! History doesn't have to repeat itself! Samara, remember when you were Lucinda for that short time. You were happy, weren't you? You liked being good, right?"

Samara stopped then, tilted her head and laughed.

"Lucinda? That pathetic excuse of a sister? Why would I want to be her?"

"But..."

"Enough! I woke up from that coma to accomplish my mission. My mission was to kill all those that stood in my way or were pathetic excuses for humans. When I fell off the cliff, two of those

127

pathetic excuses survived. My pathetic excuse for a best friend, Joyce Offey, and my pathetic excuse for a brother, Trey Jordan!"

She laughed again and started toward him, pointing the knife at him.

Trey's leg had been crushed a year ago and it had not improved since the day it was crushed, but he bravely charged at Samara, barely using his crutch. He howled in pain at the pressure he had put on his bad leg, but he had succeeded in pushing Samara into an awaiting grave, making her drop her knife. Trey picked it up, making sure it did not slip from his fingers. There was so much mud on it now that the blade was far from clean, even the blood on it before looked spotless compared to what it looked like now.

He pointed it at Samara who was fuming and grumbling, wiping mud and rain from her face. She tried crawling out of the grave, but the mud was too slippery for her to climb out.

"No!" she screamed.

Trey didn't know whether to throw the knife at her or not. It would be easy to miss her. But as he was contemplating, Samara gave a strained moan as she pulled herself up, out of the grave. Trey pointed the knife at her determinedly, hoping to scare her off.

'But I won't,' he thought miserably. 'If Lucinda didn't scare her off last time, I certainly won't.'

She charged at him, missing the knife, and put her weight on his shoulders.

He moaned at the pain his leg was giving him, but he swerved round so that Samara was the nearest to the cliff. She clung onto him tightly, as if she held on for so long, Trey would finally lose his balance and go plummeting down the cliff, just like his little sister had a year ago.

But with all his might, he pushed Samara off. Samara was thrown to the edge of the cliff. She gasped as she began to lose her balance and then gave a piercing scream as she fell to her death. The death she was supposed to meet a year ago, the death she shouldn't have escaped from.

Trey sighed. His leg was throbbing and stung as if it had caught fire, but that didn't matter. Samara was dead. She would never hurt anyone again. Backing away from the cliff, relieved but dumbfounded and the knife still in his hand, he looked back to see if his crutch were lying anywhere. But the slippery mud proved too much for him too, as he slipped and fell back. His head bumped against something. A gravestone? It hurt so much, he could not make any noise because the blow was so surprising, so painful, that he fell unconscious.

Chapter 13

"Trey?" called a voice.

Trey opened his eyes. It wasn't a voice he recognised.

"Who...who are you?" he asked a mysterious girl that bent over him. She had long honey coloured hair and blue eyes, but they were cold, unemotional, yet her voice sounded concerned.

He noticed that he was in a bed. But was it in his own bed? His own room? He didn't know? How had he got there? Why did he feel this so bad? His head and leg throbbed like crazy. He moaned as he tried to sit up.

"No, no. Don't do that," the girl said, putting her hands on his shoulder so he would lie back down. She made her voice sound concerned, but there were no emotion in her eyes.

"What happened? Where am I? Who are you?" asked Trey.

"Can't you remember anything from two nights ago?" she asked.

Trey shook his head.

"What do you mean? What happened the other night?"

The girl sighed.

"You have amnesia, Trey, so I'll start from the beginning. You are Trey Jordan, you are seventeen. The police found you at the cemetery, you had passed out in an open grave. I am Joyce Offey, one of your best friends from Burns High School. Do you remember there? You don't go there now obviously, but I do because I'm fifteen."

Trey shook his head in disbelief.

"Amnesia? What? How? Where am I?"

"It's okay, Trey. You're at my house; my mother and I will take care of you. You can go to college like you did before and when you come back from there, you're always welcome here."

"What do you mean? Don't I have a home of my own?"

Joyce shook her head.

"Don't you remember, Trey? Two nights ago, there was a horrible fire at your house. Your house burned to the ground, taking your sisters' lives. You got out in time but Samara and Lucinda didn't make it. I'm so sorry."

Trey shook his head again.

"Sisters? I have sisters? I mean...did have."

"Well, of course," smiled Joyce, trying to give him a warm smile, but it ended up looking like a sly grin that you'd give someone if you had just sabotaged their game so you're the one that's going to win.

Trey shuddered and she slid a photograph album from a bookshelf near her and opened it at various pages to point out his parents and his twin sisters.

"You always gave me copies of your photos," stated Joyce. "We were best friends at school. We shared everything together."

"What about my parents? Where are they? Did they die in the fire too?"

"No. They died a year ago in a car crash."

Trey blinked and shook his head as if it would bring back his memory.

"If there was a fire at my place," he asked suddenly, "then what was I doing in the graveyard?"

Joyce blinked, searching her brain for an answer. A believable answer.

"You were upset, Trey. You nearly lost your mind. When you realized Luce and Sam weren't going to make it, you screamed and ran to the graveyard, searching for your mum and dad's grave, crying that you had failed them because you promised to look after them when they died tragically. You weren't paying attention and fell into a new grave. It was raining that night; it's a good thing you didn't drown. In fact you might've done if I hadn't come to the rescue."

"What do you mean?"

"I was there. You called me to tell me that your house was on fire and I came as soon as I could. I had called the fire brigade and came to check to see if you were okay. You were sobbing as the firemen went in to save Luce and Sam, but they couldn't. I ran around ages looking for you in the graveyard and when I found you, I called my mum and we brought you here. It looked as though you took a nasty bump on the head; you're lucky you woke up at all!"

Trey shuddered.

"But it doesn't matter now. As long as we know now that you're alive and well."

She nodded over to a dark corner of the bedroom. Trey strained his neck to see what she was nodding at, but she ushered for him to get some rest and said she'd be up soon with a bowl of hot soup.

Trey sighed and let his head sink into the pillow.

Joyce smiled at the thing she saw in the corner again and Trey shuddered. Joyce seemed nice and she had explained what had happened, but Trey couldn't shrug off the feeling that she was hiding something, that she had something she wanted to keep secret and not just about him and his family, but about herself. Her story just didn't seem to add up.

When she smiled her cold smile, her eyes seemed to glimmer like sun had shone on ice for just a moment.

Trey moaned to himself. He had amnesia? How had he got that? From just a bump on the head? But Joyce said it was a nasty one and he had known people to lose their memories by bumping their heads. He racked his brains to remember, but there was a wall that blocked those memories and Trey sensed that that wall was there for a good reason. What had happened two nights ago, really? Did his parents really die in a car crash? Did his two sisters really die in a fire? Did he really go insane and go running around the graveyard in the pouring rain, searching for his parents' graves so that he could apologize to them what a bad guardian he was? What even caused the fire? ...If there was one. But why wouldn't there have been one? Why would Joyce lie?

He reached out for the photo album Joyce had shown him earlier and he flicked through it. The fire and everything Joyce had described brought back no memories, he had no recollection at all, but looking at the pictures, he recognised the faces, the names.

"Sa...Samara," he breathed, looking at one of his sisters with long brown hair and an unhappy face.

He could tell which one was called Samara! This was good! Or was it? He narrowed his eyes, concentrating so hard on why he had known that, but as much as he tried he couldn't. He sighed and dropped the photo album on the floor. Not remembering was so frustrating! He sighed again and let his eyes shut. He fell asleep dreaming of a girl with long hair and a knife in her hand...

Joyce was downstairs, stirring the tomato soup that she was going to serve to Trey. Of course

137

her mum was not with her like she had told Trey, she had been killed. Not by Samara, by her. She had killed her mum and dad a few weeks before Samara killed hers. She had a sister, Karen, who was eighteen and like Trey, spent most of her time in university. No one knew she lived alone because no one knew her parents were dead. She had hidden them in the attic. They sat up there like two prized statues that Joyce went up and admired sometimes. Her curly blonde haired mother in her pretty flowered frock, her face covered in a transparent bag that Joyce had suffocated her with. Her father was as cold and distant in death as he was in life. Joyce had not bothered to kill him brutally, she knew he would not give her a kick out of it. He would've probably just sat there, watching her stab him to death or something like that. She had poisoned him and that satisfied her enough. How surprised he was when he realized he was going to die from his wife's cooking! Ha! Joyce had always said her mother's cooking would be the death of them!

She put the soup to her lips and sipped it, thinking of the circumstances concerning Trey and what had happened since Samara had killed her friends, family, and Lucinda and woke up from the coma. Maybe she'd tell him one day. Maybe she'd just leave it to him to find out by himself. Maybe then she could kill him. She grinned to herself and stroked the scar on her stomach. She would've died that night if that man had not come by and called an ambulance. She had woken up in hospital, then a week later she insisted she was fine. The doctors were unsure but they let her go. On her way out, Joyce spotted Trey! Unconscious in bed. Apparently, he had been found in the cemetery in an empty grave. He had been found with a knife in his hand. Joyce understood immediately what had happened and she explained to the doctors she was a cousin and wanted to take him home so she could look after him, just like he did with Lucinda. She spun a web of lies she could tell Trey to prevent him from remembering, just like he did with Lucinda...well, *Samara.* The hardest part to explain would be her mother not being there all the time. Oh well, she'll make up something...

She turned her head round and saw a dark haired girl holding a knife in the darkest corner of the room.

"That's right," breathed Joyce. "Live in the dark in death as you did in life, Sam. You'll make sure I do right, won't you? You'll keep an eye on me."

Chuckling to herself, she poured the soup into a bowl and carried it upstairs.

Trey was asleep again. She smiled that cold smile of hers and put the bowl on the bedside table. One day he'd remember. He'd remember like Samara did, and when that day did come, Samara and Joyce would be ready...

Copyright © 2019 by Crazy Ink
www.crazyink.org

Publisher's Note: This is a work of fiction. Names, characters, places, and incidents are a product of the author's imagination. Locales and public names are sometimes used for atmospheric purposes. Any resemblance to actual people, living or dead, or to businesses, companies, events, institutions, or locales is completely coincidental.

Book Layout © Crazy Ink

13592343R00082

Printed in Germany
by Amazon Distribution
GmbH, Leipzig